Here are other novels you may enjoy
by Henry Holt Books for Young Readers

LIFE RIDDLES *by Melrose Cooper*
MAKE LEMONADE *by Virginia Euwer Wolff*
BLACK WATER *by Rachel Anderson*
PHOENIX RISING *by Karen Hesse*
THE BIG BAZOOHLEY *by Peter Carey*

Life Magic

MELROSE COOPER

Life Magic

HENRY HOLT AND COMPANY
NEW YORK

Henry Holt and Company, Inc.

Publishers since 1866

115 West 18th Street

New York, New York 10011

Henry Holt is a registered
trademark of Henry Holt and Company, Inc.

Published in Canada by Fitzhenry & Whiteside Ltd.,
195 Allstate Parkway, Markham, Ontario L3R 4T8.

Library of Congress Cataloging-in-Publication Data
Cooper, Melrose. Life magic / Melrose Cooper.
p.   cm.
Sequel to: Life riddles.
Summary: Crystal's strong family helps her deal with being put in a
remedial reading class and discovering that Uncle Joe is dying of AIDS.
[1. Learning disabilities—Fiction. 2. Family life—Fiction. 3. AIDS
(Disease)—Fiction. 4. Uncles—Fiction. 5. Afro-Americans—Fiction.]
I. Title.   PZ7.C78746Lg 1996 [Fic]—dc20   96-10567

ISBN 0-8050-4114-1

First Edition—1996

Printed in the United States of America on acid-free paper. ∞

1   3   5   7   9   10   8   6   4   2

With much love to John Muehlbauer

Life Magic

1

I was sure happy to say hello to autumn. Not that I didn't like summer, mind you. But this particular year, summer was a roller coaster. A good-bad, up-down, back-and-forth ride, like my sister Janelle had said.

She's the smart one. Even got a few of her stories published in magazines when she was just thirteen years old.

Roxann's real quiet. She's the baby, and I mean that like it sounds. Mama finally gave up trying to get Roxann to stop sucking her thumb.

Except for being in the middle, I never did know quite where I fit in. Till the magic touched my life. Life magic, I call it.

But getting back to that summer, it had been one thing after another. Janelle got famous.

Mama lost her job. Daddy came home after being gone a whole year, separated from Mama, and got a new job. And we were a family again.

It was good. And bad. Because it was different. Lots of new rules. That's why I was glad to start school. Or thought I was, till I actually got there.

See, it all started with my sixth-grade teacher. Wanted me to be tested. Said I might have some reading and language delays. That's how she put it.

Mind you, I had never been a shining star in school like Janelle, but I got by. Mama made a big deal about the A's I got on last year's report card to make me feel good. But two of them were in gym and music and the other was for spelling.

So in October, Miss Ross sent a note to my parents. Through the mail, like maybe she didn't trust me to give it to them or something. Said I needed some kind of testing for reading.

Daddy said, "Ain't nothin' wrong with your readin', girl. You just got to do more of it, is all."

Janelle said, "We could start a chapter book

tonight, Crystal, if you want." That meant that she'd read a page, then I'd read a page, and so on, and she'd have to help me with the big words. I knew she was trying to be kind, but I felt mad at her for saying it all the same.

Mama sighed. "Better to find out if something's wrong now rather than wait. Might as well have you tested." She smiled, but I knew her teeth would've shown a lot more if I had told her I got an A on a book report or won an English award like Janelle instead.

Maybe Miss Ross was wrong, I thought. I decided to let my strong points defend me. "What about spelling?" I asked Mama. "Stupids don't get A's in spelling."

Mama shook her head and sighed again. "Crystal, nobody said anything about being stupid. Anyway, spelling may be a totally different function. I've known people who can write but can't spell and people who can spell but can't write."

Roxann just sucked her thumb and tended to her new twin dolls, Dennis and Denise. Our Aunt Barbara, who lives upstairs, gave them to her for not crying the first day of first grade.

Right about then, I was wishing my thumb

and I were best friends, too. I decided I couldn't wait to ask Aunt Barbara's opinion of getting tested. She was always full of what she called life riddles, little sayings she made up or picked up from other places.

"I'm going to Aunt Barbara's," I said and hurried out before anyone could give me a chore.

Aunt Barbara was making beaded earrings for her friend Ophelia's birthday. They worked together at the public library.

I told her the story about Miss Ross's letter and she said, "There are worse things, and you know, Crystal, sometimes when one door shuts, another one opens."

Before I had a chance to ask her what doors had to do with reading and language delays, she asked, "Gold or silver?" and held up the earrings she was making for Ophelia.

I looked at the hooks. "Silver," I decided. "The beads are blue and white and gray. Silver goes better."

"You're right," Aunt Barbara said. "You've got an artist's eye for color."

"Sure, Aunt Barbara," I said. She didn't know

I was just okay at art, too. I always tried avoiding the subject around her because she was so good at it. Some of her weavings and other crafts had won awards at local shows. Like my uncle Joe the artist. He was her and Mama's brother. He used to say I had talent, but that was when I was little, and he lived out of town now.

When I got back downstairs, Daddy and Mama were playing Scrabble. Roxann was pretend-reading to Dennis and Denise. Janelle was in our room, writing in her journal. My whole family, doing word things. Just what I needed!

Janelle looked up. "Want to start a book?" she asked. "I just checked out two new ones."

I was hoping she had forgotten. "Uh, sure," I said because I couldn't think of an excuse fast enough.

She opened a book called *Sweet and Sour Lemons*. The title reminded me of the plaque on Aunt Barbara's kitchen wall that says, "When life gives you lemons, make lemonade."

"You suppose it's about that, making something sweet out of something sour?" I asked.

"Won't know until we read it," Janelle said, sitting up straight. Her eyes had that twinkle they always get when she begins new books. New *experiences*, she calls them.

I stared at my sister till my own eyes teared. I wondered if anything would ever make *me* gleam so bright.

≈ 2

They did the testing. I had to go down to Mrs. King's room three days in a row. I didn't mind on Wednesday because that was music class. But Thursday was another thing. That was gym, and we were jump roping. I didn't mind on Friday because that was only science review and I was interested in the weather chapter anyway, so the facts were already stuck in my head.

What I minded most was Lamar Wilkes, the new kid. Some of the kids were afraid of him. He was always starting fights or picking on people, seemed like for no reason. When he took the attendance to the office on Thursday, he saw me duck into Mrs. King's room. Soon as I saw him see me, I knew I was in for it.

Sure enough, at lunch he asked me, "How come you were at Mrs. King's?"

"Just because," I said. Darn, I thought, I should've come up with something better before.

"I don't know anybody who goes to Mrs. King's just because," Lamar said.

"Oh yeah?" I snapped. "Well, now you do." I felt proud of myself.

Then Lamar smirked, real nasty, like he knew something. And I got a chill like when Leon Rivera scratches his fingernails on the chalkboard just to make everybody shiver.

Meanwhile, during the wait for the test results, my family made sure I was reading up a storm. It was like October had suddenly been named Crystal's Reading Reform Month. *Sweet and Sour Lemons* turned out to be a decent experience, just like Janelle said.

Plus, Roxann made me read every night to Dennis and Denise. She was the one who actually liked the snuggling at story time, but I didn't mind pretending. Only thing I really minded was reading the same books over and over. And over.

Mama said that repeating was good for kids that age because that's how they learn. "That's fine," I said. "And they're good books, long as you hear them once or twice a week."

But Roxann insisted, and pretty soon I was reciting those stories like my own name and address. And sometimes my head played tricks on me at night and kept saying them over and over when I was trying to get to sleep.

So one day I really got tired of the same stories, and when I was browsing the library shelves to find material for my praying mantis report, I came across a book called *Big Bugs and Beautiful Beetles*. Turned out I fell in love with it like Roxann did, so I didn't mind reading it over and over. The pictures were great, too. Life-size insects crawling on everyday things, looking like they could jump right off the pages in a blink. I stared and stared at them. And sometimes I thought they moved. Honest.

I decided I might be an insect expert when I grew up. Entomologist, it's called. I only know that because Ophelia told me when I checked out the book.

Daddy thought he was real clever about helping with my reading. "Crystal," he'd say, "I don't have my glasses. Could you read me the dose on this medicine label?"

Or it would be "Could one of you girls check the *TV Topics* and tell me what's on at nine?"

and I'd just happen to be the one next to the newspaper pile.

Mama and Aunt Barbara were the only ones acting sensible about it. One day I heard Mama say to Aunt Barbara, "Nothing's going to change in a week or two. Better find out first what's what, then do whatever needs to be done."

"Readin' can't hurt her, though," said Aunt Barbara, "even so."

"That's true enough," Mama said before they went on to talking about the patients at Mama's new hospital job.

The reading part was okay with me. It was the finding out what's what that had me scared.

*E*very time I thought about the testing, I felt like a rock had plopped *splat* into my stomach. Three whole weeks dragged by like lazy slugs while I waited for the results. Then three things happened all in one day, the first Friday in November.

Mrs. Durphy, the music teacher, picked Roxann to sing a solo for the primary grades' Christmas play. I wondered for the life of me how someone shy like Roxann would ever be able to pull it off, but she did like singing. Come to think of it, Roxann liked anything to do with music, so she'd probably be just fine, long as she kept her thumb out of her mouth.

And Janelle won another prize. This one was

second place for best nonfiction article in the whole school.

She was her usual excited self when she broke the news at suppertime. "And guess what! I get to miss school to go to the Convention Center for the recognition ceremony. And I even get to have lunch with the author and illustrator who are presenting the awards!"

Aunt Barbara was down for dinner because it was her day off and Daddy's turn to work late at the hardware store. She had surprised Mama with a glazed ham and scalloped potatoes.

Aunt Barbara laughed and said, "Janelle, take a breath, will you, and tell me who the author is." Being a librarian, she was always interested in that kind of thing.

Janelle mumbled, "Not sure," and went to get her backpack while she was still chewing a mouthful of ham.

She pulled out her invitation and gave it to Aunt Barbara.

"Marsal White!" Aunt Barbara exclaimed. "She wrote *Big Bugs and Beautiful Beetles.* She's right from around here, you know."

"No, I didn't know," Janelle said.

"Crystal," Roxann whispered, but Aunt Barbara's voice went on louder.

"Her son Broward White illustrated the book. It's fabulous. Have you seen it?"

"Crystal," Roxann said a little louder. I almost swallowed a ham piece whole. When I didn't answer, Roxann exchanged her fork for her thumb.

"No," Janelle said to Aunt Barbara. "I haven't seen it. I'll be sure to, though."

I didn't say a thing. I could feel the anger turning my coffee-with-cream-colored cheeks V8 red. "No fair!" I wanted to scream, but I couldn't. It was like all the energy was stuck in my burning face. *I'm* the one who loves that book, and *she* gets to meet the author and the illustrator. Figures.

I silently went to my backpack, then came back and slid the book across the table to Aunt Barbara. She looked at me funny, like she couldn't believe I knew about it. I went to my room before she could say whatever it was rolling around in her mind and trickling down to her tongue.

Even when I put my earmuffs on, I could hear her and Mama oohing over Roxann because of the solo and aahing over Janelle's writing award. The mind keeps hearing what the ears block out.

The third thing happened while I was doing my long-division homework. I glanced up to think about what nine into eighty-two would be when there was Mama at my door, motioning me to take off my earmuffs.

"Cold?" she asked.

"Nope," I said. "Just concentrating is all."

She believed me and said, "Mrs. King called this morning just before I went to work. Just like Miss Ross suspected, your testing shows a few problems. Nothing really drastic."

Mama smiled and made her voice go up. "You'll be going to Mrs. King's remedial reading class three times a week, starting Monday. All that means is that you'll be getting some extra help with your reading and language skills."

Skills? I wanted to laugh out loud. Instead I asked, "How long do I have to go there for?" I made my own voice sound braver than I felt.

"Well . . ." Mama hesitated. "Just for this year, and then we'll see."

"Oh," I said and quickly asked, "What's nine into eighty-two?"

I wasn't good at expressing myself. Mind you, if that was Janelle being told remedial reading class, she'd sure shriek out, "Skills!" in a laugh. Then she'd sob with her face all crinkled up, right in front of anybody at all. Not me, though. No way.

I wrote down Mama's answer, but looking at the paper was just my way of not crying till she was away from my door. I just kept looking at the numbers and saying them in Spanish over and over in my head. I really had to concentrate, since the numbers were the only Spanish words I knew. Learned them from watching one of Roxann's TV shows. It stopped me from thinking what "remedial reading class" really meant for me, especially once Lamar Wilkes found out.

Later in the tub, I let the tears run down the drain fast as my shower water could wash them away.

When I got into my bed, Janelle was writing in her journal, like always. Roxann was breathing softly in her sleep, her thumb barely touching one side of her mouth.

I went to sleep, glad that tomorrow was the weekend.

I didn't know yet about the fourth thing. It happened on Saturday morning.

≈4

I slept late like I planned. No reason for me to get up. No celebrating on my part. Just plain worry, thinking about Monday and that remedial reading class.

Besides, my homework was done from the night before. I wished I could sleep the whole weekend away. Matter of fact, I was wishing I might catch some sleeping sickness and not wake up for ten months. Then Mama and Daddy'd be so glad to see me, they wouldn't even mention school.

Only reason I finally did get up was because the carrying-on woke me.

I peeked into the kitchen. Daddy, Mama, Aunt Barbara, and my sisters were group-hugging and jumping around like African dancers. I got that feeling Mama calls déjà vu. It was just like when Janelle got her first author's check and when we found out that Daddy was coming home again.

Mama saw me and motioned me over. "Crystal," she cried. "Your uncle Joe's comin' back!"

"Really?" I started jumping with them, too.

Uncle Joe was cool. He never forgot anyone's birthday and always made his own cards. He'd gone to California when I was five, and been back to visit only four times. Mostly we got to know him from his letters and from what Aunt Barbara and Mama told us.

I had a few memories of Uncle Joe, all good. He was the one who taught me to make snow angels. I hate the cold. Always have, even when I was a well-bundled baby. Every time Shawna, my best friend, says, "Let's go ice skating on Delaware Park Lake" or "How about sledding at Gunther's Hill?" I make up excuses. And then she gets mad because she has to go with her brother Kevin. And Janelle takes Roxann out to make snowmen, not me.

But somehow the cold wasn't so bad when Uncle Joe got me out in it. Now, all of a sudden, I was wishing for snow.

Best of all, he had a nickname for me. Miss

Crys, he called me. Nobody else ever called me anything but Crystal.

"When? When's he coming home?" I asked.

"Next week Saturday," Daddy answered. "Want to pick him up at the airport with me?"

"Yeah!" Janelle, Roxann, and I chorused.

While I was gulping down some Wheat Chex, I listened to Mama and Aunt Barbara making plans. "I'd better get my spare room fixed up," Aunt Barbara said. "Won't be spare for long."

"You mean Uncle Joe is staying here?" I asked.

"Uh-huh. Right upstairs with me till he finds his own place," Aunt Barbara said.

"Let me give you a hand with the furniture," Daddy offered, sipping the last drops of his coffee and sliding out from the table.

Janelle said, "I'm going to write Uncle Joe a welcome-home poem."

Roxann mumbled with her thumb half in, half out, "I don't remember no Uncle Joe."

"'Course you don't, baby," Mama told her. "You weren't even talking when he left and you're barely out of kindergarten now."

"Roxann," I said, "wanna help me make a welcome-home sign when I get back from

Shawna's?" I figured it might make her feel more included.

"Okay," she said.

After breakfast I walked the two blocks to Shawna's building, strutting like a proud peacock all the way, just from being so happy. When I got there, Shawna's mother said, "You're in fine feather today, Crystal." I laughed, thinking about the peacock, and told them the news.

Shawna asked, "Why's your uncle Joe coming back here?"

"'Cause here is home, I guess," I answered.

"But I thought he loved California," she said.

"He does," I said. "But maybe he loves here more 'cause it's where his family is." I hadn't thought to ask Mama or Daddy or Aunt Barbara why Uncle Joe was coming back. That sounded right, though.

Shawna had a dancing class at one o'clock. I walked to the corner with her, then she went to the studio for her lesson and I went home. The last two recitals she had done solos, she was so excellent at tap. Seemed everyone I knew was a winner.

The November sky was gray as steel. The last few leaves clung to the trees, looking lost and shivery. The wind kicked up, and I got shivery, too. I shoved my hands into my pockets and zipped my jacket up to my chin.

Thoughts started swirling in my brain like the fallen leaves doing reel dances with the wind. Janelle would tell Uncle Joe all about her writing prize. Roxann could share her singing. Uncle Joe would be proud of Aunt Barbara and her new art projects. Mama and Daddy would tell about their jobs. And then me, I'd have to say how I was in remedial reading.

All of a sudden, the day looked just like I felt. I was lonelier than a playground in the wintertime.

$\approx$ 5

I went to Mrs. King's class on Monday. Didn't want to, mind you. Didn't want to at all. But Miss Ross gave me a schedule soon as I sat down at my desk. I figured if I made any trouble, things would be a hundred times worse. For one thing, Lamar Wilkes would find out. Then everyone would know that I was both stupid *and* bad. If I kept quiet, maybe no one would notice. That notion flew out the window soon as I got to that first remedial reading class.

Mrs. King made a big deal out of introducing me to everyone. I already knew Eartha Gray. She was in Shawna's dance class. Shawna was in Mr. Bartlett's regular classroom in school, so she didn't know about me leaving the room for all that testing, and I didn't bother telling her. Now she'd find out for sure.

There were four other kids besides Eartha. Three boys, named Daniel, Sharif, and Justin. And a girl named Colleen, who I thought was a boy at first because her straight red hair was cut so short.

The class didn't seem like any remedial reading to me. Mostly we played games and talked about what neighborhoods were made of. Before I left, I peeked out the door real quick to make sure Lamar Wilkes wasn't walking by at that particular moment.

At recess that day, Shawna and I were hanging out by the mural wall, the one that the sixth grades painted with sports scenes, when Eartha came running up.

"How'd you like your first class at Mrs. King's?" she asked. I didn't have a chance to think of a good answer, so I didn't say anything.

"Wasn't the neighborhood exercise fun?" She was talking like I was interested or something. I didn't answer again, but she didn't seem to notice.

I kept looking at the ground. "Eartha, come on!" Tameeka Jones called from the blacktop. She was holding one end of a long jump rope.

"Coming!" Eartha yelled. "See ya," she said to Shawna and me.

I knew my cheeks looked like V8 juice again. I made designs in the dirt with my foot. I was mad at Miss Ross. Mad at my parents. Mad at Mrs. King. Mad at Eartha and maddest at Tameeka for not calling her to jump rope sixty seconds sooner.

"You go to Mrs. King's?" Shawna asked.

I stayed silent as a butterfly.

"How come you didn't tell me, Crystal? I never keep secrets from you. Best friends don't."

Times like this, Aunt Barbara says, "I wish I had a portable hole that'd open up and suck me away." I knew exactly what she meant.

First, it was almost impossible to explain what they were all calling my learning disability. According to Mama, the test results showed there wasn't really any simple name for what I had. Mrs. King had told me, "You're a real puzzle, Crystal. We can't put you into any specific category like we normally do with most kids." Aunt Barbara said that's how I could have a learning disability and still love to read.

I didn't understand it at all. Made me mad enough, though. Having a disability was bad enough, but being different on top of it set me fuming. Now I was mad at Shawna, too, wishing *she'd* drop into a portable hole instead of me.

"What was I supposed to do, Shawna? Brag about being a dummy? Huh? How would you like it if it was you?"

I stormed away. Luckily the bell rang, so I just kept stomping into my classroom and slid into my seat. I was panting hard. Had to take some deep breaths to get my breathing under control.

I hate my life, I thought. Here I was in remedial reading with a proud uncle coming home who would find out about me and get unproud soon as he did. And now, no best friend to talk to about my problems if I wanted to.

I looked out the window. The sun was shining, and I was mad at it, too. Made my eyes water, it was so bright.

"Crystal?" Miss Ross was saying.

What planet am I on? I wondered.

Barry Mallon poked my back. "Page twelve, science book," he whispered.

I scrambled for the page.

"Crystal. Today, please." Miss Ross was tapping her foot.

"Chapter two," Barry whispered.

I started reading about tarantulas. I slowly read through three paragraphs and Miss Ross called, "Anthony, continue please."

Whew, I thought. Good thing Lamar Wilkes doesn't sit behind me. He'd be giving me the wrong page just to make a fool of me.

I turned around. "Thanks," I said to Barry. He nodded and smiled real kind, like he knew how it felt to be caught thinking of something else when the teacher calls on you.

His smile made me feel like crying. Sometimes that happens to me when I'm bluer than blue. All it takes is someone to be nice to me and *bam*, my emotions bubble up like a pan of hot-cocoa milk.

But I turned off the bubbling real quick, like always. I sure wasn't going to cry in class or even look like I wanted to. That's all Lamar Wilkes would need to see.

≈ 6

Saturday morning at our house was crazier than Rich Stadium during a Bills game, with everybody hustling and bustling over Uncle Joe's arrival.

I was the only one who got to go to the airport with Daddy to pick him up. Roxann had a cold and was all whiny because she couldn't suck her thumb and breathe at the same time. She'd been awake half the night, and Mama said she had to stay put, since the day was so nasty.

Janelle got a phone call early from Mrs. James in Shawna's building. She wanted Janelle to baby-sit for her two kids, Ethan and Mavis, while she went to work because her usual sitter called in sick.

It didn't take us long to get to the airport.

What took long was the parking and walking to the terminal.

When we finally got there, we learned that Uncle Joe's plane was twenty minutes behind schedule. Daddy picked up a magazine and sat in one of those yellow chairs with little TVs attached at the ends. I stood at the huge windows, watching the planes go in and out.

I never realized how gigantic they were till now, seeing them right up close. Never flew yet in my life. My heart started pounding when I heard the roar of a jet engine, like thunder. I wondered for a second if it sounded so loud inside and decided it probably didn't, because on TV they always show folks talking and watching movies on airplanes. Nobody'd be able to hear.

Suddenly Daddy was behind me, saying that Uncle Joe's flight was in. We walked to the place where he'd be coming through. There was a crowd waiting.

Soon people started entering the doorway looking for faces they recognized. A man in a suit. A tall black-as-jet woman with a newborn in her arms. Two little Asian boys holding a flight attendant's hands. A dark-eyed girl, looked like maybe she was in college, holding a sign that said M. PAPADOPOLOUS. Probably an exchange student, I figured. And a tall thin man with a beard and the twinklingest eyes, smiling wide right at me.

"Uncle Joe!" I cried. He hugged me and Daddy at the same time.

"How was your flight?" Daddy asked when we had all let go.

"Great, thanks," Uncle Joe said.

Downstairs, we waited for Uncle Joe's suitcases on the luggage rack that spun round and round. I pulled the handle of the one that had wheels attached. Daddy insisted on carrying both the others.

We got to the doorway, and as soon as it opened, Uncle Joe shivered, zipping his thin jacket and hugging himself. "Good old Buffalo," he sighed.

"I'll pull the car up. You two wait here," Daddy said. He set down the suitcases and ran to the parking lot while Uncle Joe and I stayed inside.

"So tell me, how's Miss Crys?" he asked.

The shivers disappeared when I heard him say that. "Fine, just fine," I said. There was gray in his beard that I didn't remember from last time.

"How's school?" he asked. My heart skipped a beat. "You teaching those teachers a thing or two?"

"School's okay," I mumbled, looking down.

"Just okay?" he said.

"Bad." There. I had told the truth. I wasn't planning on saying anything at all, especially not right here in the airport terminal doorway. Maybe it was better, though, getting it over with right away.

He lifted my chin and said, "That bad, huh?"

I got that feeling like when Barry Mallon told me the page number. I swallowed hard and looked at a jet coming to land, and the tears stayed back where they belonged.

"I got tested," I blurted out to give my mouth something to do besides tremble. "Now I go to remedial reading class."

❧ 7

I waited for Uncle Joe to say, "Oh, that's too bad," or look uncomfortable or something. Instead, he put his head back and laughed a rich, deep laugh that made me want to run away. And I would have, except that he was bear-hugging me at the same time.

I felt my cheeks burning and Uncle Joe said, "I knew we were soul mates, Miss Crys. From the start, there was something special about you, far as I was concerned."

Daddy pulled up in the car. A taxicab honked at him from behind like he owned the spot. I jumped in the backseat fast. Daddy opened the trunk and he and Uncle Joe dumped the suitcases in, then they got into the car and Daddy said, "Now to get out of here. Anyone good at mazes?"

I stared at the back of Uncle Joe's head. He and Daddy were busy reading signs, so I didn't talk, just bit my lip, hoping they'd find their way soon so I could ask him.

Soon as Daddy found his route, I said, "What do you mean, soul mates, Uncle Joe?"

"No one ever told you about my math genius?" he said.

Now it was Daddy's turn to laugh. I frowned, looking from one of them to the other.

Uncle Joe said, "When God was making my brain, He left out the math part. I can't add two and two, you know."

"Uncle Joe," I said in a scolding tone.

"Okay, okay, that's an exaggeration, but it's not far off. I've got a genuine handicap. I guess these days they call it a learning disability. Difference is, when I was going to school, there weren't any special classes for kids like me."

"What did you do?" I asked.

Uncle Joe twisted around in his seat to look back at me. "Suffered through," he said. "Got called lazy by my math teachers, especially in high school, till they saw how well I did in other subjects."

"Like art?" I said.

"Art?" he laughed. "No way! In fact, that's how I found out I could draw. Taking chemistry in senior year."

Uncle Joe had my head in a spin. "What in the world does chemistry have to do with art?" I asked him.

"I had this one teacher, Mr. Denny, who believed in me, that's what," he said. "You see, I was so frustrated taking those chemistry tests, I could have hit someone or something. It was like a foreign language to me, didn't make any sense whatsoever. Once, all of a sudden, I started doodling when I couldn't figure out the answers. And my doodling turned out to be some pretty decent drawing. I never knew I had it in me until that very moment, no lie." Uncle Joe crossed his heart and went on.

"But once I did, there was no stopping me."

"Didn't Mr. Denny get mad when you handed in drawings instead of chemistry answers?" I asked.

"Get mad? This is the best part, Miss Crys. Not only did he not get mad, he asked me for more drawings, believe it or not. He actually stood right in front of the whole class one day and said, 'Joseph, I think you are destined for great things, but chemistry isn't one of them, I'm convinced.' He told me to try. That's all, just try my best. And I did. He even gave Marvina Moselle extra credit for tutoring me after school."

"I think he was trying to play matchmaker there," Daddy said.

"You're probably right," Uncle Joe said. "And Mr. Denny told me to keep drawing him pictures because they were a pleasant diversion from all the facts he had to check."

"Wow!" I said. I couldn't imagine Miss Ross being that understanding. Then again, I didn't have any special talent like Uncle Joe. "Did you pass?"

"By the skin of my teeth, with a sixty-five," he said. "And I think Mr. Denny searched high and low for enough points because he understood what nobody else did—that I *did* try, I just couldn't do it, pure and simple."

"So your life changed just like that?" I snapped my fingers.

"Right. Like magic. Things happen like that sometimes if you just let them," Uncle Joe said.

"And," Daddy added, "if you're lucky enough

to be in the right place at the right time, with people who are just letting them happen."

"You two sound just like Aunt Barbara now, with all her life riddles," I teased.

"It's true, though, Miss Crys. Just when you think you're heading in one direction, the wind can blow you the other way before you can blink. It's kind of an abracadabra thing."

An abracadabra thing, I thought, wishing some of that magic would happen to me. Then I caught a glimpse of my face in the rear-view mirror. My eyes were gleaming bright as Janelle's when she gets that new-book look in them.

Uncle Joe's coming home is magic in itself, I thought a split second later.

An abracadabra thing.

~ 8

Mama and Aunt Barbara were absolutely wild to see Uncle Joe, jumping around and carrying on like they do. Uncle Joe stayed downstairs so we could all eat dinner together. Afterward, Aunt Barbara hung around to help with the dishes, but Uncle Joe was tired and wanted to get to bed.

"Here," said Aunt Barbara, handing him the keys to her place. "You're so jet-lagged, you can hardly keep your eyes open."

Uncle Joe did look tired. He didn't apologize for going up early, just said, "Thank you all for a marvelous homecoming."

He was right next to me when he got up to go, so he gave my head a touch. I grabbed him and gave him a huge hug around the waist. That wasn't like me at all, mind you. Don't know what came over me. It was like my arms just shot forth with a mind of their own. Uncle Joe bent down and said, "Good night, Miss Crys," and gave me a forehead kiss.

Soon as he left, I felt disappointed. I thought he'd stay down and play Scrabble and Boggle for hours, like last time he was home. But tired is tired, and bed is where he wanted to be.

Right away Mama said, "He's a shadow of himself, did you notice?"

"Sure did," Aunt Barbara agreed. "Thin as a starved garter snake."

Daddy added, "That was the first thing that struck me when he got off the plane."

"Well," Aunt Barbara told Mama, "between your cookin' and mine, girl, he'll be rolling out the door soon enough." We all laughed.

"Did you guys all get along that well when you were growing up?" Janelle asked.

Mama and Aunt Barbara started shrieking with laughter.

"What's so funny?" Roxann took her thumb out long enough to ask. She was breathing better already. Good thing. Maybe tonight she'd fall asleep instead of whining like last night.

"Like hyenas and zebras, they got along," Daddy joked.

"Oh, hush," said Mama, pretending to punch his arm. "You weren't even there."

"You've told me plenty of stories, though," he said. "Remember when he hid on you two when you were baby-sitting and how you got back at him? The girls might enjoy that one."

Mama and Aunt Barbara rolled their eyes at each other. Roxann and Janelle and I begged to hear the story.

"Oh, all right," Mama said. She leaned against the countertop. "Aunt Barbara and I were in junior high. Uncle Joe was a second grader. Well, you know how those silly rumors in grade school get started? There was one about aliens."

Aunt Barbara interrupted. "Nieces, first you've gotta be told that Uncle Joe wasn't always the best of brothers. Once he hid on us, like your dad said, while we were baby-sitting. Your mama and I were frantic, searching every-where, asking neighbors, the whole bit. Finally, she spotted his sneakers poking out from under the living room drape. Of course, that was ten minutes after your grandma, God rest her, had come home from work and found him missing with us in charge."

"So we were grounded, and it wasn't the first time, either," Mama broke in. "He was always pulling tricks like that because we weren't allowed to punish him. He took advantage of the fact that he was Grandma's baby." My head and Janelle's snapped over in Roxann's direction.

"What about the aliens?" Roxann wanted to know.

"Oh yeah, go ahead." Aunt Barbara waved at Mama to continue.

"Like I was saying about the rumors, spaceships were supposedly on the way to Buffalo to capture every fourteen-year-old girl with light brown skin. But first, in order to fit them all into the spaceships, they would zap them with ray guns and turn them into tiny pills. So one day, your aunt here and I devised a plan."

Mama fake-bowed and gestured with her hand toward Aunt Barbara, so she took over. "We picked Uncle Joe up from school as usual, making sure to talk all about the spaceships like we were scared to death as we walked on home. We kept looking up at the sky."

"Then," Mama said, "Aunt Barbara fed him a snack while I went upstairs and changed my clothes. I snagged one of Grandma's aspirin tablets from the medicine chest and drew a frowny face on it with a ballpoint pen. Then I left it on top of my pile of clothes I had just changed out of and sneaked over to my friend Charmaine's next door."

Mama and Aunt Barbara's laughing kept interrupting the story, making it longer.

Aunt Barbara continued. "Pretty soon the phone rang, as I knew it would. I had a mouthful of cookie, so I mumbled to Uncle Joe to answer it. He did, and it was your mama on the other end, calling from Charmaine's house. Only he thought she was calling from the alien spaceship. Tell them what you said." She motioned to Mama.

Mama sung out in a spooky, faraway voice, "Help, Joey. Help me. The aliens . . . they've got me. They're turning me into . . . oh no, I'm a tiny pill! Help!" Then the phone went *click*.

Mama and Aunt Barbara were doubled over and howling, remembering it.

"What happened?" Janelle and I asked at once.

"I told him to look in our bedroom," Aunt Barbara went on. "Our sister must be there, I told him. Well, he saw that aspirin tablet and freaked out big time."

Mama said, "Sure did. He was still doing those little after-cry gasps when Grandma came home an hour later, even though I had come back and proven to him that I had escaped from the alien ship."

"And you were dead meat, right?" Janelle said.

"Deader than chopped sirloin," Aunt Barbara said. "And grounded for two weeks with no reprieve."

"And it was worth every minute," Mama said.

"Was Uncle Joe a better brother after that?" I was curious.

"I'd say," Mama recalled, "he started treating us with a little more respect."

"R-E-S-P-E-C-T." Mama and Aunt Barbara started singing and dancing to that Aretha Franklin hit. Then they did their shrieky laugh again, and it passed on to us like chicken pox through a first-grade classroom.

I wondered if Janelle and Roxann and I would ever go crazy over memories like that and dance around one of our kitchens while our children looked at us amazed.

I kind of hoped so.

9

Everybody was so happy that Uncle Joe was home. "That's how it oughta be with family," Aunt Barbara always said. "If God intended families to be apart, He'd have given us passports and airplane tickets right inside our mothers."

That's why it was so weird when the mood changed. In a finger-snap, too, it happened. I remember the exact day.

It was the second Monday after Uncle Joe came home. I remember it so well because that was the day Lamar Wilkes made fun of Roxann after school on the playground.

"Baby, baby, stick your thumb in gravy," he sang.

If I want to call Roxann "baby" and tell her to get her thumb out, that's one thing. But let

45

anyone else make fun of my sister, that's another story.

"Lamar Wilkes," I said, "why are you always knocking other kids? You got a problem or something?"

At first Lamar Wilkes was shocked that I even faced up to him. (Tell you the truth, it surprised me, too.) His eyes got wide and he stared at me hard. But then he got his mean, narrow-eyed look and said, "At least I don't go to a retard reading class."

If Uncle Joe hadn't come home before that statement and given me cause to be happy, I would have probably burst out crying and never gone back to school again. And if Uncle Joe hadn't told me about his learning troubles, I would have felt like a total worthless nothing. But now remedial reading class was like the cold not being so bad when Uncle Joe and I made snow angels.

"Come on, Roxann," I said. "He's not worth arguing with." I held her hand and we walked toward home from the playground, calm and dry-eyed as you please.

When we got home, Mama's eyes had that

puff underneath that was there whenever she wanted to cry but tried to hide it from us. Aunt Barbara seemed moody. Her voice was low and slow, reminding me of a tape stuck in a cassette player. Daddy was slouched over, as if he'd been lifting heavy boxes all day.

I found my older sister in our bedroom.

"Janelle," I whispered. "Something's up."

"You're right," she agreed. "But I can't figure out what it is yet. I already asked, and they all said they're just tired."

It's true, I know, that tired can put a puff under your eyes and a slouch in your back and trade a good mood for a bad one. But I had a sense that whatever was doing this to three adults at once wasn't plain old tired, mind you.

"Remember when Daddy came home and everybody got tense? Remember Aunt Barbara said there's always a period of adjustment when folks come back home?" I said.

Janelle sighed. "Know what, Crystal? I'll bet you're right. It's the adjustment, that's all."

I felt better. Like Aunt Barbara says, "Good or bad, stress is stress, and it always makes a mess."

"You seen Uncle Joe today?" I asked.

"Nope," Janelle answered. "Aunt Barbara says he's got a bad cold and a skin rash."

"Shoot," I said. "I hope he's better by Thanksgiving."

"He probably will be. It's three whole days away," Janelle said. "And you know how grown-ups are."

"Yeah," I said. "They don't stay sick for long."

Uncle Joe *was* better. Thanksgiving came and went. Roxann was a smash at the Christmas play in mid-December. I don't know when I've ever been so proud of her. Then it was all hustle and bustle, buying gifts and wrapping them and cooking with Mama, Aunt Barbara, and my sisters. Uncle Joe didn't get fatter, though, even though Mama and Aunt Barbara tried feeding him like he was a show pig getting ready for the county fair.

The Saturday we had a great snowfall, a tug came early at my bedspread. "Miss Crys, get up and look out the window, would you?" Janelle stirred, and Roxann's thumb popped into her mouth.

Everything was white, far as I could see.

"Snow!" I cried quiet as I could. I scrambled for my clothes.

"I'll grab some coffee while you get ready," Uncle Joe whispered.

He was warming his hands on the mug when I slid into another chair in the kitchen and poured myself a bowl of Cheerios. I crunched them plain (it's a cereal I like better without milk). Mama was mixing meat loaf for supper. She was up because today was Daddy's Saturday to work.

"Let's go," I said, downing the last handful.

We sneaked down the steps. I was glad my sisters didn't wake up. I hadn't had Uncle Joe to myself since the airport, what with school and everybody else and the painting he said he wanted to do.

We fell onto the patch of front yard, fanning our arms to make wings. We made as many angels as we could, then moved on to the next building's front yard.

We got up to admire what we'd done. "Too bad our footprints leading up to them have to be there," I said. "They sort of spoil it."

"And what would you suggest we do to eliminate them?" Uncle Joe asked.

"Can't," I admitted. "It's just too bad we can't drop down out of the sky and just make them, like real angels, is all."

He laughed. "Yeah," he agreed. "Too bad."

The air was crisp but calm. Uncle Joe went into a coughing fit. "Still got that stubborn cold," he spluttered between coughs. By the time we got done with our second patch of angels, Uncle Joe's teeth were chattering like a rattlesnake's hind end.

I teased, "Boy, this sure is a switch. I'm the one usually gets cold, and you're the snow lover. See what happens when you become a California boy?"

"Yep," he agreed. "I guess I've turned into a warm-weather wimp. How about some hot cocoa and a cream doughnut?"

"Race you to the doughnut shop," I said, taking off like the wind.

It was the first time I ever beat him. Uncle Joe jogged lazily along. I waited at the door.

"That cold is really slowing you down," I remarked. He just panted and nodded.

I ordered for both of us and Uncle Joe paid.

We sat in a window booth and watched the huge snowflakes that had started to dance in the air like soft feathers. Right then Shawna walked by on her way to her early-morning recital practice. I knocked and waved. Shawna stopped for a second. Then she waved and smiled, too. Lucky Shawna doesn't hold grudges. Whenever we fight, we never actually make up. We just sort of start talking again after a little while and things are fine.

"Your dancing friend," Uncle Joe recalled. He had only met Shawna once. That's another thing I liked about Uncle Joe. He always paid attention.

We slurped every drop of our cocoa, licked the cream off our fingers, and walked home slowly.

The sun came out as we reached our building, so bright I had to squint just to see where I was going. The new snowflakes looked like jewels on our snow creations.

"Look at the angels," I exclaimed. "They're glistening."

That sun was so bright, it made Uncle Joe's eyes tear like crazy.

≈ 10

March came, acting lion-fierce and lamb-gentle, like usual. My birthday was the twenty-fifth.

"What do you want for your birthday?" Mama asked me two weeks before the date. "I've been saving to take us all to dinner."

"All of us? Even Aunt Barbara and Uncle Joe?" I asked.

"Yes," she said. "And I was thinking that maybe you could ask Shawna, too."

"Sounds great to me!" I said. "Can we go to Manchurian House?" I love Chinese food.

"We can go wherever you want. You're the birthday girl."

The day came, and I was excited. While we waited for our order, I opened my gifts. Shawna gave me heart earrings. Mama and Daddy gave me two sweaters and a pair of jeans. I got a new backpack from my sisters, the very one I had shown them at the mall right after Christmas. Then Janelle said, "I've got another gift for you. Here." I opened up a book that had no words written in it.

"Crystal, it's a journal, for writing in," she explained.

"Oh," I said. "Thanks, Janelle."

I didn't know if I meant thanks or not. Did Janelle think she could solve my reading and language problem by trying to turn me into a writer like her?

I almost said that out loud, but then I looked at her. Tears were running down her face. "Janelle," I said instead. "It's nice. Really. Thanks a lot."

"You're welcome," she said. Then she excused herself and went to the rest room.

"Shoot," I said. "Janelle doesn't think I like her gift at all. I've gone and hurt her feelings."

"That's not it at all," Mama assured me, looking weird at Aunt Barbara.

The waiter brought out bowls of steaming food. "Chicken and snow peas. Um, um!" I exclaimed.

A few minutes later Janelle came back from the rest room, looking fine. She noticed Roxann's sweet-and-sour chicken and remarked, "I'll bet you order that because the chicken pieces are shaped like thumbs."

Shawna and I laughed and Uncle Joe scolded, "Girls, that's enough, all of you. Older ones shouldn't tease little ones. I know how *that* feels." But you could see his mouth was working to keep the smile off it.

Daddy made a big deal out of the fortune cookies. His fortune said "Lucky in love." He raised his eyebrows to Mama, and she did it back.

Mine said "Your star shines brightly," and Shawna's said "Talent lies deep within you and is yet to be uncovered."

I frowned. "Here, Shawna, let's trade." I exchanged our tiny bits of paper. "Now it's right. You're the one that's the shining star."

Mama gave a big click with her tongue, the way she always does when she's annoyed with me. I don't know why she should have been annoyed, though. Mind you, I was only telling the truth about having no talents. Come to think of it, maybe that is the reason she had her tongue clicking.

The restaurant folks surprised me with a cake, burning candles and all. Soon as the waiters walked through the swinging kitchen doors, my family started singing "Happy Birthday."

I decided that this was my happiest birthday ever. I tried taking it all in, like my mind was a camcorder or something, so I could replay it every time I needed a cozy, warm feeling.

Back home, we watched a movie on Aunt Barbara's VCR because we didn't have one. Anyway, part of the birthday plan was a sleepover in her apartment for just Shawna and me.

Aunt Barbara waited till the movie was over. "Crystal, gift time," she announced.

"Aunt Barbara," I protested. "The sleepover is my gift."

She waved her hand and put the remote on Stop. "The big box on the table is yours. Happy birthday."

Shawna followed me into the kitchen and helped me tear the wrapping off. We both gasped when we saw what it was. "Aunt Barbara! A VCR! You're too much. Thanks!"

The only one who hadn't given me a gift yet was Uncle Joe.

Shawna and I lay on sleeping bags on the living room floor. We stayed up talking till one in the morning. We probably would have talked longer, except Aunt Barbara stuck her head around the corner and said, "Hey, you guys, will you give me a break? One o'clock is late enough, even when you don't have school. And I have to work in the morning."

"Sorry," we whispered.

Shawna had to get up early, too, for recital practice. I felt a little sorry for her. But like she said, it didn't kill anybody to spend the day tired once in a while.

Uncle Joe slept longer than I did after Aunt Barbara and Shawna had left. I loved the snuggle-down, sleep-in feeling. It was eleven when I finally got up and went to have some breakfast.

Just as I finished my last bite of waffle, Uncle Joe strolled into the kitchen. He was carrying something big and flat, wrapped in a blanket. "Happy birthday, Miss Crys," he said, sliding it carefully on the table in front of me. "I wanted you to see this all by yourself first."

I closed my eyes till I had it all uncovered. Then I stared.

"Oh, Uncle Joe," I whispered. The words barely came out. All my breath was gone from gasping when I realized what his gift was. "One of your oil paintings."

"A special one," he said.

I looked closely. It was a picture of me and my sisters in the snow. Janelle and Roxann were building a snowman in one corner. I was in the center, making a snow angel. Uncle Joe was up in the sky, looking down on us, mostly at me. He was surrounded by light and—I peered harder—had wings.

"What do you think?" he asked quietly.

I hugged him and said, "It's beautiful." Then I giggled. "But Uncle Joe, you're not a real angel. At least not yet."

I looked at the painting some more and then up at him. His eyes were all teary, but there wasn't any sunlight today. I gulped. "Uncle Joe, what's wrong?"

That's when he told me he had AIDS.

≈ 11

Something happened to me then. It was like I was a VCR and someone pulled the plug. I just shut off for a while.

Janelle would have been sobbing for sure. Roxann, too, besides sucking up a storm with that thumb. But not me, mind you. I felt like I did right before I had my tonsils out in third grade when the doctor gave me a shot to make me drowsy. Calm, real calm. Numb all over.

"How do you know?" I said to Uncle Joe, just as casually as if I was asking him what time it was.

"Blood tests," he said with a gulp. He was still trying to swallow back his tears.

"There was a show on TV the other night," I remembered. "Talking about false positive AIDS tests. That's probably—"

Uncle Joe interrupted me. "There's no false about this. I wish there were."

"Look, Uncle Joe," I said. "Doctors are just people. They're not God. Doctors make mistakes."

Uncle Joe got up from his chair and came over to me. He gripped me by the shoulders and looked at me straight on. "Miss Crys, I'm dying."

I looked away. Uncle Joe kept right on saying what he needed to. "I told the rest of the family already. I just couldn't find the right oppor-tunity to tell you. But you need to know. My last blood test wasn't good, honey. If I get sick again. . . . Well, it's time you knew."

I should be crying, I thought. I ought to be feeling the whole world caving in on me. But I didn't feel anything at that moment, bad or good. Nothing at all.

There was a knock at Aunt Barbara's door. Janelle. "Mama wants to know if you two are hungry. She's making grilled cheese sandwiches for lunch."

"I just ate breakfast," I told her.

"I wouldn't mind a sandwich, long as you have sweet pickles to go with it," Uncle Joe said.

"Sure do," Janelle replied. "You know, you and Mama have the same tastes in food."

With a sweep of his hand, Uncle Joe moved toward the door and said, "Ladies."

I picked up my painting and followed Janelle out while Uncle Joe locked the door behind us.

I went right to my bedroom and set that painting against the wall, facing in. I sunk onto my bed and thought about things.

Somewhere in a far-off world I could hear people laughing in the kitchen. Laughing and joking as if there was something happy going on.

Suddenly it all made sense, things that happened before that didn't seem to fit but did now. Like how Aunt Barbara and Daddy and Mama changed after Uncle Joe got home. It wasn't the adjustment. It was AIDS all along.

That was why Janelle left my birthday table crying. Not because she thought I didn't like the journal. Only because she already knew what I'd be needing to write in it.

And Uncle Joe didn't have just a normal cold and a rash before Thanksgiving. He had something that AIDS was causing. That's why he wasn't getting any fatter, either, even though

Mama and Aunt Barbara were doing their best to fill him up.

I knew the signs. We learned about AIDS in health class. And anyway, Monique Bailey's older brother died of it just last year. She's a senior in high school and lives in Shawna's building. She came into our school and told us the stuff you don't learn in the textbook and handouts, like how the rest of the family feels.

I can remember thinking, Poor Monique and lucky me. Thank heaven I don't have to think about AIDS.

Maybe I don't just have reading and language delays, I thought. I had life delays, pure and simple. How could I have missed it? I should have been able to add up two and two. Or maybe it's like Aunt Barbara says, "We only see what we want to see. Our eyes just blink out the overload."

Worst part about me was the feeling delay. Something bad must really be wrong with me, I decided. I mean, my uncle had just told me the hardest thing in his life, and I was acting like I plain didn't care.

That lonely wintertime playground feeling started creeping through me, like a draft through a hallway when someone's left the door ajar. Suddenly I felt chilled to the bone.

I curled up on my bed and didn't realize how sound asleep I had fallen till Roxann was saying, "Crystal, wake up. It's suppertime."

I smiled at her. For one blessed second, I had forgotten. But when I remembered the morning, I felt like there was a long, dark tunnel I had to get through. Trouble is, I had no energy for crawling through it.

❧ 12

*E*very time I looked at Uncle Joe, I wanted to shout, "Uncle Joe, I care! I really do. I hate that you have AIDS." Somehow I couldn't tell him, though. Couldn't think up the words to match the feelings, when it came right down to it. And when I did think of the right words, they stuck in my throat like too much peanut butter. So whenever I was around him, I sort of acted like everything was normal, even though it's not how I felt. Not at all.

I told Shawna the week after Uncle Joe told me. She put her hand on my arm, real gentle, and said, "Oh, Crystal, I'm so sorry. What can I do to help you?" in the tone Barry Mallon used that day in school. That tone that got my eyes to tearing worse than the brightest sunlight.

Next few months, I was like a soda bottle being shook up, ready to explode.

Uncle Joe had a few bouts with sickness here and there, nothing real serious, though. "He's holding his own," Aunt Barbara said. But deep down, I knew the truth. One of these days he'd get sick, and there'd be no getting better.

Like that soda bottle, I'd keep fizzing up. Then just before the bursting point, I'd fizzle back down again, just in time. Didn't take much to get me fizzing, either. One little shake was all.

Like the day Daddy said, "Crystal, please help Roxann with her bath," when I was in the middle of social studies homework.

"I'm not your slave!" I shouted. "Or hers! She's old enough to take her own bath. Everybody around here babies her so much, it makes me sick!"

Daddy closed my door and I heard the water running, so I figured he must be helping Roxann himself.

A few days later, Janelle asked me if I'd seen the book she'd been reading for her book report. I yelled at her, "How should I know where it is? I'm not on your reading level; I

64

wouldn't touch it. What do you think I am, anyway, your own personal librarian or something? Keep track of your own books, why don't you?"

She just stared at me. Then she shook her head and left the room.

Seemed like whenever Shawna was around, I got into fights with her, too. She started not calling me so much. And we used to talk every day.

Same with Aunt Barbara. I got tired of her witty remarks. Why couldn't she just talk normal like other folks?

And Mama, *she* was driving me craziest of all. "Do this. Don't do that. Make your bed. Put your laundry away. Don't forget your reading assignment. Wear your hat. Go to bed early tonight. Are your teeth brushed? Got any homework?"

I felt mad at everybody all the time. Couldn't help it. I especially felt mad at Lamar Wilkes. Turned out, he was the shaker that finally caused my soda bottle explosion.

We were in spelling one day, learning the words by repeating them over and over. Modern as Miss Ross was in lots of ways, that was one old-fashioned thing she believed in. Rote memorization, she called it.

Eighth word on our list was *retarded*. A couple kids started smiling, till Miss Ross gave them her look. So everybody else started spelling R-E-T-A-R-D-E-D correctly. Not Lamar Wilkes, though. Mind you, his voice shouted out loud and clear above the others, "C-R-Y-S-T-A-L."

Some of the boys started laughing. Miss Ross folded her arms and started to say, "Lamar." But I beat her to it.

I swirled around so fast, I must have left cloud puffs like cartoon characters do. "Who do you think you are, you stupid fool?"

"Crystal!" Miss Ross warned. But I wasn't done.

I wished I could say something clever, but I just screamed at him. "I'm sick of you! Sick to death!"

My last word was drowned out by the screech of Lamar's desk as I shoved it, hard as I could, sending him sprawling backward onto the floor.

"Crystal!" Miss Ross screamed, running to Lamar's side. "Are you all right?" she asked him, looking back at me like I was a rattlesnake prepared to strike a second time.

I stood there panting. The whole class was frozen with their mouths hanging open.

Soon as Miss Ross found out that Lamar was all right, she said through clenched teeth, "To the office."

Lamar fixed his desk and sat down with a nasty smirk on his face. I spun around to go. Behind me, I heard Miss Ross say, "Both of you. It takes two, Lamar, and you're the other half."

I walked, slow as I could. Took the long-cut clear around the building. No way I was going to be anywhere near Lamar Wilkes.

The principal was waiting at the door when I got there. "Hello, Crystal," she said, like maybe I wasn't in trouble or something. "Come in."

Lamar must have walked even slower than me because he got there second. "Lamar," Mrs. Pinto said like a greeting. She gestured to her inner office. "Have a seat, each of you."

We sat. "Who would like to speak first?" she asked.

Lamar Wilkes and I shut our mouths tighter than clamshells. I felt my face burning. I looked at the floor. There was a jagged scrap of ripped-out spiral notebook paper lying there. It reminded me of a white bird flying. Sometimes splotches on our linoleum bathroom floor do that, too, look like other things. I kept staring at it. Out of the corner of my eye, I could see Lamar's one knee moving up and down real fast.

"Well?" Mrs. Pinto said.

I raised my eyes half an inch. Her long, pink-polished fingernails were clicking on her shiny desktop.

I pretended that paper scrap turned into a huge dove and flew me right out of Mrs. Pinto's window. Then I thought I'd better change that dove into a gull or a pigeon because a dove is a symbol of peace. And there sure wasn't any of that around.

13

Amazing things happened that day that I never could have thought up in a million years, even if I was writing a make-believe play.

One was that Mrs. Pinto just sat there clicking her fingernails like she had all the time in the world to do nothing but click. Just sat there waiting, that's all, till one of us talked.

Drove me crazy, so I just blurted out, "I'm sick of Lamar Wilkes always making fun of people." I started rattling off the times he teased Roxann in the playground, and me at Mrs. King's and all. Then I felt like crying. Last thing in the world I wanted to do. I managed to gulp back the tears before they got anywhere near the running-down-my-cheeks stage. I was getting good at it. I was getting a headache, too. Always did when I stopped the tears.

"Lamar," said Mrs. Pinto, "does any of that sound familiar to you?"

Lamar's knee was still jerking up and down. Started going faster even, soon as Mrs. Pinto talked to him.

I thought he was going to smart-mouth her, but he didn't. He said, "Yeah, it does," in a voice so soft I couldn't believe it came out of Lamar Wilkes.

Mrs. Pinto said, "Sometimes when something is on a person's mind, that person can be angry and confused. And sometimes those feelings make that person lash out at others, whether they have anything to do with the problem or not."

I thought about how I'd been treating Shawna and my family. But how did Mrs. Pinto know that? I felt like she had X-ray vision into my soul.

"Tell you what," Mrs. Pinto said. She opened up a door on a little tan refrigerator that looked like the safe in the hardware store. She took out two cans of cherry soda and flipped the tops off. I almost laughed, thinking of me being a soda bottle with all my fizzings and explodings. She handed one can to me and one to Lamar.

"You two cool down for a while. I have a few phone calls to make. Mrs. Lopez is right outside the door if you need anything." She shut the door and left without another word.

I knew it! I thought. She's calling my house. I couldn't remember if it was Mama's day off or Daddy's late day. "Please, oh please, don't let anybody be home," I prayed silently.

Suddenly I realized how dry my mouth was. I took a big sip and swallowed so hard, it hurt my chest. I could hear Lamar slurping some, too. But I wouldn't even glance in his direction.

Out of the blue, he said, "I can't believe how you pushed that desk."

"Me neither," jumped out of my mouth before I had a chance to remember that I wasn't talking to Lamar Wilkes ever again, long as I lived.

"What's making *you* so mad?" he asked.

And just as quick, I answered him again. "My uncle's sick." I sure could have used some of those language delays now, I thought, but the words just flew out.

"I hear he has AIDS," Lamar said. "That so?"

"Maybe, maybe not," I said. "And anyway, it's none of your b——"

Before I got out the word *business*, Lamar interrupted. "AIDS killed my mother," he said, matter-of-factly like maybe he was saying "It's ten-thirty" or something.

I snapped my head up and stared straight at him. He acted like I didn't believe him. "In the summer. That's why I'm new here. Had to move in with my grandma."

Tears sprang to my eyes without any warning. Big ones, racing down my cheeks, not the kind that trickle slow and easy. I gulped. "Oh, I'm sorry, Lamar. You must miss her. Did she suffer much?"

Soon as I said that last part, I was even sorrier. Real sorry. But I was thinking of Uncle Joe. Feeling terrified.

Lamar said nothing and I was out of words. We just stared at each other.

I was still staring at him when the most amazing thing of all happened.

Lamar's lip started quivering. He took a sip of soda real quick to stop it, but it didn't work. His face crunched up like a used tissue. His shoulders shook, and loud sobs started making him choke.

I didn't know what to do. I thought that I

shouldn't just sit there, so I stood up and took the soda can from his hand. I set it, along with mine, on Mrs. Pinto's shiny desktop.

I wanted to clamp my hand over his mouth. I didn't know what to do about the sobbing. Lamar's tears were so big, they plopped like huge raindrops onto the front of his shirt. A couple even fell right to the floor. He didn't even try to hide them. Just sat there with that scrunched-up tissue face.

It was horrible. How was I supposed to act in this situation? What would Mama do? I asked myself. Or Aunt Barbara? Or even Janelle?

And suddenly without another thought, I put my hand out and touched Lamar on the shoulder. Quick as a blink, he stood up. And before I knew it we were hugging. Me and my worst enemy, Lamar Wilkes, hugging like lovey folks, right in the middle of the principal's office.

And neither one of us tried to pull away, even when Mrs. Pinto opened the door.

I started spending more time with Uncle Joe. Some days, we'd talk and talk. Other days, I'd watch him sketch or paint.

I thought Uncle Joe's hands were like magic

wands. After all, he had even said that art happened in a magic way for him. An abracadabra
thing. He'd wave them, and scenes would come
alive. Whole stories, you might say, with set-
tings and moods and characters.

"Drawing and writing aren't so different, are
they?" I said to Uncle Joe.

He turned around and looked at me like I
had just solved a chemistry problem in my
head. "Hmm." He nodded. "I guess they are just
variations on the same theme."

I watched his magic-wand hands create some
more, amazed at how they could make a flat,
dull surface come so absolutely alive.

⤳ 14

Somehow Lamar and I had become friends, doing a lot of talking and spending a lot of time together. Janelle said, "It's a misery-loves-company thing." But I like Aunt Barbara's explanation better. She says, "Enemies become friends paired when simultaneous feelings are shared."

The months passed. Soon it was June, time for Shawna's dance recital. "Mind if I bring a guest?" I asked when she gave me my ticket. "Sure, but I'll have to get another ticket, and they cost five dollars," she said.

I went to the box where I kept my allowance. "Make it two extra," I told her, giving her a ten-dollar bill.

"All right." She eyed me suspiciously. "I'll bring them to school tomorrow."

"Thanks," I said. One ticket was for Uncle Joe.

Right away, Lamar said he'd go to the recital with me, and Leon Rivera overheard him say it. In gym, some of the kids were chorusing, "Lamar and Crystal, sitting in a tree, K-I-S-S-I-N-G."

Didn't phase me one bit. "This soda bottle's all fizzed out," I said to them. They looked at me like I had just dropped down from Jupiter, as Janelle would say.

What did I care that they were saying that? I had somebody new to do things with this summer, especially when Shawna went to her grandma's in Kentucky for two weeks like she did every year.

On the way to the recital, Uncle Joe stopped to pick up flowers for us "to give to our star," he said. I felt jealous for a second when I heard that. Nobody'd ever call me a star for anything. But seeing Shawna dance took my mind off all the bad feelings. You couldn't feel anything but amazed and proud watching her do those complicated steps, making it look so easy. When it was over, we all clapped till our hands were sore.

Afterward, we went backstage and gave

Shawna the flowers. Mrs. Davis asked us all to come back to their house for cake and ice cream. Uncle Joe said, "Thank you. We'd be delighted."

I'll always remember the way the sunset looked that night. We were on Shawna's balcony, just me and Shawna and Lamar and Uncle Joe. We talked about the orange and pink and yellow and coral all blending.

Uncle Joe was saying art things, talking about how it would make a good watercolor wash and such.

"If you ask me," Lamar said, "it's just plain pretty." We all laughed.

I wanted to gobble up that orange and pink and yellow and coral moment, gulp it down and keep it inside me forever.

Then suddenly my thoughts turned to something else. "Uncle Joe. You're about two hours overdue for your medicine."

"That occurred to me," he said. "But we can let it go, just this one time."

"You sure, Uncle Joe? Maybe we ought to leave," I said, sounding like Mama.

He smiled and said, "You know, there's an old

African proverb, one of my favorites, that goes like this: 'He who is too careful with his own life will be killed by a falling leaf.' "

"Where'd you get that one?" I asked. Soon as I said it, I realized.

Shawna, Lamar, and I blurted out at once, "Aunt Barbara!"

Uncle Joe threw back his head and joined us in our laughter.

I'll never forget the sound. Our voices were as orange and pink and yellow and coral as the sunset. And the feeling spilling over us was just as warm.

≈ 15

Uncle Joe was right. Missing the one dose of medicine didn't hurt him any. Matter of fact, he was so good all summer, I started believing he wasn't even sick at all.

Uncle Joe painted like there was no tomorrow. I still watched him a lot. Sometimes Shawna and Lamar watched with me. We sat there, silent as butterflies, in the same room, but probably in different worlds of thought.

In July, Uncle Joe showed his work at the Orchard Park Art Festival and won a ribbon for *Watching Over You*. That was the angel painting he had done for my birthday. He asked if he could borrow it. Of course I said yes.

I felt proud at the art show when folks recognized me from the painting. Three people asked about buying it, even though Uncle Joe had put a SOLD sign on it the very first day. Two of them settled on other pieces when Uncle Joe convinced them that he absolutely, positively would not negotiate, no way, no how.

A few weeks later, Uncle Joe took me and Lamar and Shawna to Albright-Knox Art Gallery. We made a day of it, with a picnic right on the grounds.

"Did you bring your medicine, Uncle Joe?" Shawna asked. By now she and Lamar called him that, too.

"Got it right here." Uncle Joe laughed, touching his pocket. "Good thing I have you guys to look after me." He poured a paper cup of lemonade and took his pills. Not that he needed them anymore, I thought.

I gazed up at the blue sky and thought about the winter days of dazzling sunlight and about the gentle sunsets of June and couldn't decide which I liked better.

Uncle Joe and I took a train ride to Pennsylvania and back for a whole day, just to say we did it. We came home tired, but feeling satisfied, just in time to see some fireflies twinkling in the shrubs under our building.

"Oh, how I've missed the Pennsylvania scenery," he said, as he sat on our front stoop.

"I didn't know you were ever there before today," I said. There was always so much to learn about a person, once you start knowing him, I thought.

Uncle Joe gave me a faraway smile. "My friend Allen's godmother lived there, in the country. Auntie Addie, we called her. We took the train to see her several summers in a row. Allen could go only if he had a friend with him, and I lucked out because he was an only child."

"And you got away from Mama and Aunt Barbara." I laughed.

"That was the best part." His laugh echoed mine. "And were they ever jealous!"

"It *is* beautiful in Pennsylvania," I said.

"The hues of green—spectacular!" He sighed.

"Uncle Joe, the artist." I chuckled. "You ever see anything and *not* think of color and shadow and perspective?"

"Never!" He shuddered, like I'd just asked him to commit murder or something. "And you, Miss Crys, are starting to speak the language of art."

He brought his sketch pad when he took me, Shawna, and Lamar to the zoo the next week.

"Time out," he'd call in front of some animal's cage. And then we'd go off and find a bench or a snack stand till he finished sketching.

Finally Lamar said, "Hey, I wanna try that." So Uncle Joe gave him some paper and a pencil.

"Look," Lamar said after concentrating forever. Shawna and I had been riding the merry-go-round. Felt like old times.

"Neat!" Shawna said.

"Know what it is?" he asked, all excited.

"A parrot," Shawna and I answered at once.

Lamar frowned. "I was drawing *him*." He pointed. We leaned over to get a better look.

"That's a duck-billed platypus!" Shawna sputtered.

We were both howling and holding our sides in seconds.

"Sorry, Lamar," I gasped between choking breaths, "but I never heard of a parrot-billed platypus before."

Uncle Joe caught the drift and looked over Lamar's shoulder at his masterpiece. He said,

"Well, it appears that Lamar has created in one afternoon what evolution takes centuries to accomplish."

It was okay because Lamar was such a good sport. All the way home, we took turns saying, "Parrot-billed platypus," and hooting like hyenas every time.

It seemed that while the Fourth of July fireworks were still lighting up my mind, September came and seventh grade started.

By some amazing miracle, Shawna, Lamar, and I all got Mr. Pabst for homeroom. I still went to Mrs. King, but she said she was pleased with my progress. *Astounding* is the word she used. I was reading almost at level now. Life was looking good. No one teased me and Lamar anymore, either.

Then one night I was helping Janelle with the dishes when I heard Mama and Aunt Barbara talking about Ophelia from the library. "Can you stand it?" Mama said.

"The irony is too much for me," Aunt Barbara answered.

"What's irony?" I asked.

Aunt Barbara bit her lip like she was trying to think. "A twist of fate, you might say."

That didn't help.

"Irony," Janelle explained, "is something that happens that is totally opposite of what everyone expects will happen. We learned it in English reading O. Henry's short stories."

"The king of irony himself," Aunt Barbara remarked.

"I'll say," agreed my sister. Janelle was showing off, I knew, but it was okay. If I was smart like her, I'd probably show off worse.

"See, here's the situation, girls," began Aunt Barbara. "You know Ophelia at work? Well, here everyone was worried about her mother, who's been sick for years. And what happens? Her thirty-five-year-old brother, never ill a day in his life, goes and has a massive heart attack."

"Did he die?" I gasped.

"Just about," Aunt Barbara said. "But as luck would have it, he felt bad at work, so he made a doctor's appointment. He was on his very way to his doctor's office when, bingo, right in front of Mercy Hospital, his pains got so bad he just pulled in there instead. They put him on a heart monitor and boom, total cardiac arrest. They had to zap him with the paddles six times just to bring him back."

"That is irony with a capital I, if you ask me," Mama commented.

"It's one of those truth-being-stranger-than-fiction cases for sure," Janelle said.

I said, "It sounds like a made-for-TV movie."

After I said that, I decided right then and there that that's how it would go with Uncle Joe. Here I was, always worried about him, probably for nothing.

It didn't happen that way, though. Not that way at all. It happened the opposite of irony, and I never did figure out a word for it yet.

≈ 16

It was the middle of November. One night Janelle said, "Looks like Uncle Joe has his Thanksgiving cold and rash again."

"Just like last year," I remembered.

"And he'll be all better for Thanksgiving, too, just like last year. Just you wait and see," Roxann told us, tucking Dennis and Denise into bed.

She was a second-grader now and still loved those dolls like any mama loves her real babies, but she and that thumb had parted ways a bit. She actually got through her meals now without ever sucking it once. And two nights before, she fell asleep singing to her twins and never did put that thumb in.

"Looks like Roxann's thumb is learning to behave," I said to Janelle.

"It stays pretty busy in second grade. That's probably why," Janelle said. We both smiled at Roxann and she smiled back.

"I'll go up and check on Uncle Joe before bed," I said.

"Give him a hug from me," Janelle shouted.

"Me, too," Roxann piped up.

"I'll give him one each from Dennis and Denise, okay?" I added. Roxann loved it when we acted like they were real.

Something woke me during the night. Not a phone ringing or a door slamming. Nothing like that. Maybe a gentle tug at my covers. Or a whisper inside my head telling me there was something I should know. I never did quite figure out what exactly.

The bed creaked when I got out of it. Janelle stirred and turned over. Roxann just slept. Her hand was resting on Dennis's head, nowhere near her mouth.

I looked in Mama and Daddy's room. Their bed was rumpled, but they weren't in it. I frowned. The clock on their bedside table said 6:14 A.M. We'd be getting up in an hour. Where were they at this time of the morning?

I went to the kitchen and flicked on the light. There was a note on the countertop where we always left messages. It was in Daddy's handwriting.

J + C —
Mama, Aunt B. and I took Uncle J. to hosp. Get R. and yourselves off to school as usual. Make sure she has lunch $ in backpack. Lock up before you leave.
Love — D.

My heart rolled over in a strange way. My stomach, too. For a minute, I thought I might start gagging, I felt so sick.

"Calm down, Crystal," I told myself out loud. I paced up and down the kitchen, thinking about all the other times Uncle Joe was sick. Then a calm took me over and I smiled. He always gets better, I thought.

I yawned. Long as I was up, I might as well make good use of the time. I got three bowls out and poured some cereal in. I set our places with spoons and napkins and then suddenly remembered that I forgot to do my math homework. No wonder I woke up! I got my backpack and did the problems and was dressed before I even called my sisters.

Janelle asked, "How was he when you went to see him last night, Crystal?"

"Tired, that's all," I told her.

"Maybe it's not too serious then," she said.

"Right," I replied. "He's been sick a million times and always gets better."

"Then why is he in the hospital?" Roxann whined. In went the thumb.

"They have to be extra careful with AIDS patients, that's why," Janelle explained. "Their systems are more fragile." She sounded like some kind of professional. That was just like her anyway, trying to make us all feel better.

I poured milk in all our bowls.

"Okay," said Roxann, replacing her thumb with a spoonful of Wheat Chex.

"It's good to be cautious," Janelle added. "That way they can avoid *real* problems."

The worry was gone from her voice now. I felt better as we went out the door.

That day, Lamar and I had our first fight since

the day we stopped being enemies. It happened at recess when I told him and Shawna about Uncle Joe.

Shawna was nice and said, "I'm sure he'll be fine, Crystal."

Lamar just said, "Don't get your hopes up."

I stared at him, hands on my hips. "What kind of a thing is that to say? I thought you were my friend!"

"I am," Lamar said. "That's why I said it. You can't keep kidding yourself."

I knew he wasn't finished, but I didn't wait to hear the rest. "Come on, Shawna. Let's get out of here," I said. "I need friends right now, not enemies." We walked away.

"Besides," I yelled so Lamar could hear, "Lamar doesn't know what he's talking about." But I knew he did, I just couldn't face it. I guess I was wishful-thinking out loud.

"I hope I *am* wrong!" Lamar shouted to my back. "But if I'm not . . ."

I clamped my hands over my ears. I refused to listen to another word.

Three of our classmates were playing double Dutch. Alice and Shinetta were swinging, and Precious was jumping. I kept my mind on the rhythm of the ropes and jumped in with Precious, soon as I saw the chance.

We did one hundred and two jumps together before my foot got caught. We had just grabbed the ends for Alice and Shinetta when Mr. Pabst called, "Time."

"Tomorrow," we said as we went panting back to class.

⌒

When we got home that day, Mama was still at the hospital, but Daddy was there to tell us that Uncle Joe had pneumonia. He ended up having some serious seizures, too, over the next few weeks, but he did get better and was taking some new medicines. It was a rough month, but he made it.

There was a beautiful early-December snowfall the day after Uncle Joe came home from the hospital. He had to stay inside, but I went out and made snow angels for us both. He waved to me from the window.

"I still think the footprints spoil it," I said when I came back in. "I wish there was some way to erase them."

"Miss Crys, you are some kind of perfectionist. Only real angels can do that." He laughed in his deep, rich way, sounding healthy and strong to me.

Lamar and I didn't exactly apologize, but we made up just the same. Over and over, he said he was glad he was wrong about Uncle Joe. I said I was glad, too. And we all got back to normal.

≈ 17

As it turned out, Lamar was right after all. His timing was just off a little.

Uncle Joe died, day after New Year's. Had a seizure and hit his head against the edge of the bathtub. And died, just like that.

I was at Shawna's writing pen-pal letters when the phone rang. Saw her face go gray as she listened. "It's Janelle," she said. "There's an ambulance at your place. Uncle Joe."

I was out the door, racing home faster than I ever thought I could run. I fell smack on my face, but got right back up and ran even faster.

I reached the sidewalk in time to see the ambulance driving away. Daddy and Mama and Aunt Barbara were right behind, in the car.

Janelle was sobbing so loud, the sound was echoing off the stoop. Roxann was clinging to her with wide eyes, sucking her thumb so hard, you could see her cheeks go in and out.

"It'll be all right," I said, wrapping my arms around both of them.

"N-no, it w-won't, Crystal. N-not this time." Janelle choked her words out.

"He always gets better," I told her. "You know that."

"He's d-dead," Janelle said. And that's how I found out that nothing would ever be the same in my life again. Didn't sink in right away, though.

Mrs. Hairston, our first-floor neighbor, stroked my cheek, real gentle. "I'd better fix you up, child. Come on in, your sisters, too." She herded us into her apartment like a mother hen with chicks to tend.

Fix me up? What was she talking about? I wondered.

Soon as I sat down, I knew. Wasn't till then I realized I had left my coat and boots at Shawna's. I had run all the way home in my socks. One knee of my jeans was ripped from falling. Blood stained the rest of the leg and I had a nasty cut on my chin from when I smacked my face.

"Your uncle was a good man, girls," Mrs. Hairston said as she tilted my head back to clean my chin wound. "And so talented. We sure will miss him around here."

I think that's when it hit me. She said *was* a good man. There were tears in her eyes as she shook her head sadly, looking over at Janelle and Roxann, who were holding each other on the couch.

I shivered. Mrs. Hairston got one of her colorful afghans from the couch and wrapped it around me. My teeth started chattering like I would freeze to death, right there in her cozy living room.

Mrs. Hairston kept us the rest of that day. Tried feeding us supper that I barely remember picking at. Sometime after dark, we all fell asleep watching videos that Mrs. Hairston kept for her granddaughter. I remember Daddy leading me to my bed, seemed like the middle of the night.

I woke up the next morning, still in my ripped and bloody jeans. Mama said the wake was at Demmerlys' Funeral Home at two o'clock the next day.

She and Aunt Barbara and Janelle, they did so much crying, their eyes had that puff underneath them all the time now.

Roxann sucked till she got a thumb bump again, just after it had started getting back to normal.

Daddy went around hugging everybody, acting brave. But every now and then, I'd see his shoulders shaking from behind and then he'd disappear into the bedroom or the bathroom.

Me, I was surer than ever that something must be wrong with me. I felt empty. Just plain blank, like there wasn't anything inside me at all.

❧ 18

Right before we left for the wake, I was sitting on the couch, just staring at the rug. Aunt Barbara sat next to me and hugged me tight. Then she took me by the shoulders and looked me straight in the eyes.

"Don't worry," she said. "Everyone grieves in her own way, in her own time." It felt like she was reading my mind. "The amount of tears doesn't necessarily match the depth of the grief."

I wanted to thank her, but I didn't know how. But not knowing what to say was nothing new to me. Aunt Barbara just went back to hugging me. I think she knew I appreciated what she said, though, because of the extra-hard squeeze I gave her after she said it.

Janelle and I sat in a vacant room in the funeral home for the longest time. We were trying to put off having to look at Uncle Joe.

"When I die, I'm not gonna have a viewing," Janelle declared. "I don't want people looking at me in my coffin."

"I don't think you'll care if you're dead," I told her.

"Anyway, it's an awful custom," she started to say.

"Anyway, it's a closure. It's a good way to say good-bye and finalize things," Mama said. We hadn't heard her and Daddy come in.

"Then how come Roxann doesn't have to come?" I asked.

"She does, but not yet," Mama said. "Roxann is younger than you two. That's why we left her with Mrs. Hairston. We want to prepare her a little more and then we'll bring her right before the funeral."

"Come on, girls," Daddy said. "There's only an hour left for tonight. Let's get it over with. We'll be right beside you both."

Janelle and I stood up like robots. Mama led Janelle in, and Daddy led me.

My legs felt rubbery, but I made it. Uncle Joe

was lying there peaceful, looking asleep. Without thinking, I reached out and touched his hand. Janelle started crying, and that set Mama off again.

I just stood there staring, thinking about how those magic hands had once turned paints into lifelike things. Except for the cold feeling of his skin, it wasn't as scary as I thought.

Right after, Shawna and Lamar came in together. Shawna's mother brought them. Mrs. Davis said, "Oh, Crystal" in that kind tone. She stroked my face so gentle, and tears were threatening to jump right out of my eyes, but I gulped them back, like always. Even when Shawna and Lamar cried, I kept under control.

That night, Janelle was like a faucet that wouldn't shut off. There were no more sobs left in her, but the tears just kept running out of her constant like a summer rain. Twice, she had to dry off her journal at the heat vent before writing in it again, it got so soaked.

Roxann got two shoe boxes from Daddy and Mama's closet and pretended they were coffins for Dennis and Denise. "Make her stop!" I begged Mama. "It's disgusting."

But Mama said, "Let her be. She's preparing herself."

"I'll let her be if I don't have to look at that," I said. I grabbed a blanket and stormed out to the living room to spend the night on the couch.

It was too early to sleep, though, and I had to do something. I went back in and got that journal Janelle had given me so long ago. Maybe it's time, I told myself.

What could I write? Janelle was the writer in this family after all. "Uncle Joe died," I began. I ripped out the page. Stupid, I thought. I started doodling. Doodled some more. Drew some lines. Squiggled here and there.

I drew a butterfly. A bird. A meadow with flowers and a lone tree. And they all looked like what they were supposed to be. Not great, mind you, but it was a good start.

It was like some kind of amazing power had taken over my hands, made them perform all by themselves. Draw things I could never draw.

But I knew it was more than that. Aunt Barbara sometimes says, "Genius is often born of pain," whenever she finds out that a great writer or artist has gone through some suffering.

Now, I'll never claim to be a genius, but on a lower scale, I understood.

And sometimes it takes an alarm to give a wake-up call. That's how I thought of what happened. My talent was asleep. All these months of watching Uncle Joe at work were like a dream, and his death was the alarm that jangled me awake. Dreams and all.

I ripped that page out of my journal, too. And gently put it under my pillow.

≫ 19

Morning of the funeral, we all went early and took Roxann, just like Mama said. She did fine, too. I gave her a pat on her head to let her know. Her teeth held her thumb in place while she gave me back a little smile.

I was the last one to say my private good-bye to Uncle Joe. I reached into the pocket of my jumper and pulled out the meadow scene, then slid it down between the satin folds in Uncle Joe's coffin. "I want this to go with you," I said before I joined the rest of my family for the service.

Reverend Walter said a lot of nice things about Uncle Joe. A lot of personal, special things because he had grown up in our very own neighborhood and had gone to high school with Uncle Joe.

Everyone went to Grange Street Grille after the funeral. I spent most of the time in the front hallway. "Crystal," Mama scolded when she found me. "Where have you been?"

"I don't think it's right to be having a party on a sad occasion, Mama."

Mama rolled her eyes. "It's not a party, Crystal," she said with a sigh. "It's a funeral breakfast."

"You can call it what you want," I told her. "Looks and feels like a party to me."

"Crystal, survivors need people around them. It eases the grief," she said.

Nothing she said would change my mind. I said, "Mama, Uncle Joe's the one I need around to ease my grief, and he's not here. What I need isn't food or people, because they can't ease my grief. I wanna go home is all."

Mama did something then I never thought she'd do. Reached into her purse, opened her wallet up, and handed me some money.

"Suit yourself," she said. "Here's bus fare. Just be careful."

"Thanks, Mama."

"Can't force you to go against what you believe in," she said.

I sighed deep. Then I hugged her hard. "I'll be careful," I whispered. Then I went to the rack to get my coat.

The fresh cold air hit me like a slap. I didn't care, though. Nothing could hurt like the pain inside me. It had started taking over for the numb feeling I had before and kept growing like a toothache.

And even then, I didn't know how bad it was going to get.

✌ 20

Aunt Barbara and Mama stayed in our apartment, looking at old photo albums of when they were growing up. They did more hugging and sobbing than I ever thought two people could do. Finally Mama said, "I can't take these memories anymore. Let's try something else."

They got out the Boggle game. Shook the cube of letters and let them fall into place. Then Aunt Barbara turned the timer to see how many words they could make before the three minutes were up.

During the game, they spotted the word *Joe* at the same time. Did that ever set them off!

I wondered what it felt like to cry like that. I wondered why I was the only dry-eyed one in my family.

Daddy had gone to bed early. Not only was

he tired, but I think he knew that Mama and Aunt Barbara needed their sister time.

Roxann brought Dennis and Denise to the couch and played with them in a normal way, thank heaven. She made those shoe boxes into car seats instead of coffins this time. I didn't think I could take another night of that.

Janelle was already in our room. I think she wrote about three chapters in her journal. She was so busy blotting the tears from it and concentrating on her thoughts, she never even noticed I was using my own.

She wouldn't have believed it if she'd seen it, anyway. I didn't believe it myself. Pictures started coming out of me I never knew I had inside. A cardinal, like the one that whistles from Mrs. Hairston's window feeder. A snowman with branch arms. Shawna in her dance outfit. Even Dennis and Denise with a book between them, looking like real kids.

I held up the pages to the light. No, it wasn't a secret formula with pictures on the other side or anything. The paper wasn't magic, but whatever was happening to me sure was.

I fell asleep with the light still on and woke up with a stiff neck. My journal lay open on my lap. I squinted and saw the drawings and remembered, half dreaming, I had done them all by myself.

Wait till Uncle Joe sees these! I thought. The excitement woke me up completely.

And once awake, I remembered.

Uncle Joe would never see my pictures. He would never know that his art magic was in me, too. We would never make snow angels together and be blinded by the bright white light of winter. He would never take me and my friends for a picnic. There would never be another pink and yellow and orange and coral sunset. And no one would ever, ever call me Miss Crys again.

Now I knew why grieving folks talk about having heavy hearts. I felt like mine was a rock in my chest. A boulder maybe.

Breathing was hard to do. This grief wasn't just a mental thing. It was a physical thing, too. I ached all over, inside and out.

Suddenly I heard someone wailing. Sounded like a wolf howling, but much sadder. It got louder and sadder. I looked around. My sisters were staring wide-eyed from their beds. That's when I realized the sound was coming from me.

Mama and Daddy raced into my room. Aunt Barbara had slept on our couch, and she was right behind them. Janelle and Roxann came to my bed. And then we were all holding each other, rocking and sobbing and stroking hair and patting backs and soaking each other with tears that all came from the same place.

Last thing I remembered was Mama saying, "Stay home from school tomorrow, Crystal. The rest will do you good." She was rubbing my back, and Aunt Barbara was humming a lullaby song, and Daddy was pulling the covers up to my neck.

⤲ 21

When I woke up hours later, my sisters were gone. Usually I heard if a pin dropped in my room, but today they got ready for school and left and I never even knew. My clock said 10:21.

I could still feel the all-over ache. Wasn't quite so strong, though. My breathing came a little easier, too.

I stretched and went to the bathroom. The water felt good on my tear-streaked face. I no sooner got it dried off, though, than the tears started running again. I wiped them away with my arm and slowly got dressed. Then I went to the kitchen and tried to decide if I was hungry at all.

I pulled the curtain aside. Snow covered everything. The plows hadn't been by yet, so it was really fresh. Wouldn't Roxann and Janelle be surprised if they were looking out their class-room windows! I hope they wore their boots, I thought.

There was a peaceful look to it. Suddenly the sun came out, real strong, and everything glistened, bright as the sequins on Shawna's recital costumes.

I took a deep breath, but what I saw made it stick in the middle of my throat. It couldn't be, I told myself. Got to be my imagination working overtime for sure, I thought.

I went closer to the window. Pressed my face right against it and squinted hard at the patch in front of our building. And there it was. A perfect snow angel. And mind you, not a foot-print going to it or from it anywhere in sight.

I grabbed a sweatshirt and put it on. I crept, quiet as I could, past Mama in her bed and Aunt Barbara, on the couch, both still sleeping. The grief had exhausted them even more than me.

I turned the doorknob, quiet as a thief, and went downstairs and out to the front. I peered at the perfect snow print and a voice-memory filled my head. "Only real angels can do that."

I walked over and lay right down beside it. A warm glow spread all through me. I don't know how long I was there, but suddenly it was Mama's voice filling my ears. "Crystal, what are you doing? You'll catch your death. Get on up here this second!"

"Coming, Mama," I said. She didn't really have to worry, though. Somehow the cold wasn't so bad when Uncle Joe got me out in it.

I never told anyone about the angel. Figured they wouldn't believe me anyway, seeing that my footprints were all around by then. Anyhow, there are some things that just don't need telling.

That day, I did a lot of looking at Uncle Joe's angel painting hanging above my bed. I even talked to him when nobody else was around. Made the ache different. Like taking a painkiller for the flu. It didn't actually take the flu away, just made it easier to live with here and there till it wore off and you had to take some more.

❧ 22

Grief isn't something you *get over*. When Uncle Joe died, it was like a big black hole opened up in my life, and that hole is always gonna be there, long as Uncle Joe isn't. Because that was his space, can't ever be filled by anybody else. So I can't get over it. It's more like I've got to learn to live with it. Try to fill it up with other things, maybe make other folks happy like Uncle Joe made me.

Pretty soon after the day I saw the snow angel, I figured out *how* I could start filling up that big black hole.

I started drawing till my hand cramped. But I didn't mind. It felt good. I made cards for all my friends for holidays and birthdays and started helping kids who needed it in art classes. Mrs. Duncan, my art teacher, asked me to do the spring bulletin board. She said I was like a flower in the desert that lies around for years doing nothing, then suddenly gets a dose of rain and blossoms prettier than any other plant around. I guess that was my wake-up call theory, just said in different words.

By May, I had already won an award. First ever in my whole life. The Urban Center had a contest, which Lamar and I both decided to enter. It was for making panels for a paper quilt to honor the memories of loved ones who had died of AIDS.

Lamar drew a boy with tears coming out of his eyes, reaching his arms out to the thin air. He used a bubble, like they do in comics to hold the words, to show that the boy was calling, "Mom!"

I thought he'd win for sure, but the judges liked my angel picture better. I drew one that came right down from the sky and was hovering over a snow angel with no footprints anywhere in sight. I felt like it was a continuation of Uncle Joe's picture. My own style, though. All my own.

They called Mama and told her there would be a ceremony at the Urban Center two weeks later. She was waiting in the hall when I got home from school to tell me. She was so excited, couldn't even wait till I walked in the door.

I went to bed that night thinking about how it would be. Shawna and Lamar and my whole family would see me get an award. Shine like a star. Me.

Next day, Roxann came home from school crying. "What's the matter, baby?" asked Janelle. She was sounding more like Mama every day.

"I was supposed to get Mrs. Jackson for third grade, but she's going to have a baby and now we're getting this man, Mr. Ortiz, instead," she sputtered without taking a breath.

"Mr. Ortiz?" Janelle sounded excited. "He's coming from the magnet school. I hear he does all sorts of neat things with his classes."

"I hate men teachers. I want Mrs. Jackson." Roxann was pouting.

"Well, you know what Aunt Barbara says, don't you?" Janelle said. "When one door shuts, another one opens."

"What does that mean?" Roxann frowned.

"It means that sometimes," I told her, "things

that are magic happen to you when you least expect them to."

"Really?" Roxann said. Her crying had stopped and she took a little breath.

"Really," I said. "It's kind of an abracadabra thing."

She laughed and repeated "abracadabra" and ran off to get Dennis and Denise.

The ceremony night came.

I accepted my award and talked about who my quilt panel was for. I cried some. Let the tears roll right down, didn't try to choke them back. Didn't want any headaches ruining that night!

Like I said, my friends and my whole family were there that night. Some folks said too bad Uncle Joe wasn't there, but I knew better. Because of what happened when I was making my speech.

I looked down for a second. When I looked up again, I saw a light, bright as the winter sunshine. I felt like I was gleaming, too.

And right while I was speaking, I heard another voice say, "Good going, Miss Crys."

Some colors swirled before my eyes and turned the whole room orange and pink and yellow and coral, all blending.

A good watercolor wash.

Just plain pretty, mind you.

Magic.

Life magic.

An abracadabra thing.

Melrose Cooper was inspired to write *Life Magic* after someone dear to her lost a close friend to AIDS. As a frequent speaker at urban elementary schools, Ms. Cooper is always surprised by the number of children whose lives are affected directly or indirectly by AIDS. She hopes that writing about the subject will make it a little easier for young readers to understand a very painful and difficult illness.

The mother of six children, a granddaughter, and many pets, Ms. Cooper lives in Hamburg, New York.